HARRY HOYLE'S GIANT JUMPING BEAN

BY WILLIAM VAN HORN

SCHOLASTIC BOOK SERVICES

NEW YORK · TORONTO · LONDON · AUCKLAND · SYDNEY · TOKYO

For Elaine, Noel, and Tish

No part of this publication may be reproduced in whole or in part, or stored in a retrieval system, or transmitted in any form or by any means, electronic, mechanical, photocopying, recording or otherwise without written permission of the publisher. For information regarding permission write to Atheneum Publishers, Inc., 122 East 42 Street, New York, N.Y. 10017.

ISBN 0-590-30357-0

Copyright © 1978 by William Van Horn. All rights reserved. This edition is published with minor text changes by Scholastic Book Services, a Division of Scholastic Magazines, Inc., 50 West 44th Street, New York, N.Y. 10036, by arrangement with Atheneum Publishers, Inc.

12 11 10 9 8 7 6 5 4 3 2 1   4   0 1 2 3 4 5/8
Printed in the U.S.A.   18

Harry Hoyle was a collector. He collected all kinds of things— baseball bats, rocks, shoelaces— everything. It was his hobby.

Harry lived with his cat, Max,
in a big house at the top of a hill.
There were 72 rooms in the house.
And all of the rooms were filled
with things that Harry collected.

One room was filled with rocks.
Another room had hat racks.
And there was even a room
filled with string.
Every day Harry and Max would go to
a different room.

One room had 88,000 marbles in it.

"I love my collection of marbles," Harry would say.

"But every time I go in that room, I slip and fall on my head."

Max would look at him as if to say,

"That's your problem, Harry, not mine."

Another room was filled with telephones.
As soon as Harry walked into the room,
the telephones would all begin to ring.
The noise was awful, and it always gave Harry a headache.

"I love my telephones," Harry would say,

"but I do wish they would not all ring that way."

Then Max would look at Harry as if to say,

"What else do you expect telephones to do?"

The room Harry and Max liked the best
was the one filled with vanilla ice-cream cones.
"Mmm-mm!" Harry would say. "Vanilla is
my favorite. And nothing bad can happen
to me in here. Even if I get ice cream
on my necktie, it's all right...."

"I have the world's largest collectio

of neckties in the next room.

I can always get a clean one!"

There was one room that Harry and Max
stayed away from. It was the room where
the giant jumping bean was kept.
The room was at the very top of the house.
There were no windows in the room.
The door was made of heavy steel.
Harry kept the door locked at all times.

After all, a 50-pound jumping bear
could be dangerous.
Once it had nearly
knocked Harry and Max flat,
and once was enough.

"I hate to think
what would happen
if that jumping bean
ever got out," said Harry.
"It could wreck the whole house."
Max looked at him and shook
his head as if to say, "Then why
on earth did you ever buy such a thing?"

Harry shrugged his shoulders
and said, "It is the only giant
jumping bean in the world, Max.
I couldn't resist it."

There was one other room in the house
that Harry did not go into very often.
It made him nervous.
It was the room where he kept
all of his strange, stuffed animals.

There were gorphs, gottles, plurts, nangs, nerls,
norfs, wottles, todds, and even kitsuls.
Whenever he walked into the room,
Harry had the funny feeling that something
—maybe a wottle—was alive and watching him.
He was never sure. It was spooky.

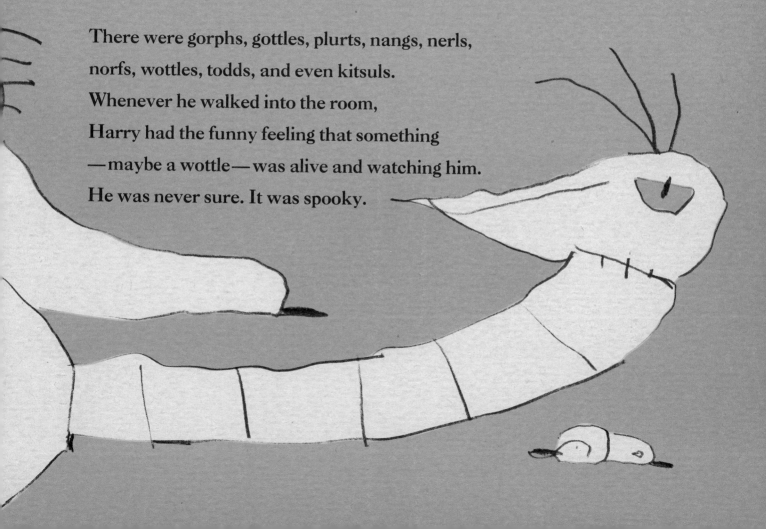

But even if some things were spooky
or dangerous or messy,
Harry had to have them all.
He added new things to his collection
year after year.

Then one day Harry saw that he had run
out of rooms.
The house was full.

"What am I going to do, Max?" asked Harry.

"I just bought a whole truckload of old doorknobs.

I have to put them someplace!

If I leave them here in the yard,

they will rust."

Max smiled in the way that cats smile.

He looked at Harry as if to say,

"How should I know?"

Harry sat down to think.
"Where can I put these doorknobs?"
he asked himself. "Where? Where?"
Then the answer came to him.
"Of course! The only room in the house
that isn't full is the one with the
giant jumping bean in it.
There's plenty of room up there
for my doorknobs."

Then Harry had another thought. He frowned.
"Before I can put my doorknobs in that room,
I'll have to capture the giant jumping bean
and take it out of the house."

Max could not believe his ears.
He looked at Harry as if to say,
"And just how are you going to do that?"

"I've got it, Max!" said Harry.

"If we wait until late at night,

maybe the giant jumping bean will be asleep.

Then we can sneak up on it and catch it with a net."

Max ran under a bush.

He looked out at Harry as if to say,

"Not we, Harry—you! I'm staying right here!"

Harry got a strong net and a heavy club.

Late that night, he tiptoed up the stairs.

He stopped outside
the heavy steel door
and listened.
There was no sound
at all from inside
the room. "Good," said
Harry. "The jumping
bean is asleep."
Carefully, he opened
the door.

Harry took two steps into the room—
and wham! The giant jumping bean leaped on him
and knocked him down.
Then it jumped through the open door
and bounced down the stairs, bumpity-bump-bump.

"Come back!" yelled Harry,
and he ran after the bean.

From room to room went the bean.

It jumped up and down and smashed everything

in its way.

First the toothpick dolls, then the model airplanes.

One collection after another was smashed and broken.

"Stop!" yelled Harry. "Stop it this minute!"

The bean paid no attention to him.

Harry didn't know what to do.

He couldn't hold the bean in his net.

And when he bopped it with the club,

the bean only jumped harder than ever.

Soon the bean was covered with ice-cream cones,
neckties, feathers, and parts of old comic books.
Harry's hat racks, his marbles, his bottles, buttons,
and barrels—all were smashed and scattered about
everywhere. The whole house shook.

Then, with one last mighty jump, the bean crashed
through the front door and bounced off down
the hill into the night.
Harry never saw it again.

Harry stood in the front yard panting and puffing.

Max came out from under the bush where he had been hiding.

He had that "sorry-I-was-such-a-fraidy-cat" look
on his face.

"Oh, it's all right, Max," said Harry. "For all the good I've done,
I might as well have been under the bush with you."
Harry sat quietly for a while.
He wondered what would become of the giant jumping bean.

He thought, too, of all those rooms full of his wonderful collections—
collections that were smashed and broken beyond repair.

But he did not cry or feel sorry for himself.

After all, Harry Hoyle was a collector.

There were a lot of other things to collect.

"We'll start all over again, Max," he said.

"And best of all, we'll have 72 large rooms to fill."

Max looked at Harry as if to say, "Only this time no giant jumping beans, right?"
Harry looked at Max and smiled.
"Right!" he said.